DIRTY DERMOT

igloo

Dermot was always dirty.

He couldn't help it. It just happened!

The harder he tried to stay clean and tidy,
the scruffier and dirtier he became.

Every morning, Dermot's mum washed his face and tucked in his clean, white shirt, ready for school.

And, every day, when school was over, Dermot was dirty again.

"I couldn't help it," Dermot began. "It just happened!"

Dermot's mum smiled wearily.

One day, Aunt Clara came to visit. She was always extremely clean and tidy. When she saw Dermot, she was horrified.

"From now on," she said, "you must stay clean and tidy. You're always so dirty and scruffy and it simply won't do."

"But, Aunt Clara," said Dermot, "I can't help it."
"Nonsense," said Aunt Clara, and sent him straight upstairs for a bath.

All that day, Dermot tried to stay clean and tidy. It wasn't easy! He went into the garden and sat on the wall.

His dog wanted to play.

"Sorry, I can't," Dermot said. "I've got to sit here and stay very still. It's the only way I can stay clean and tidy for Aunt Clara."

"Woof!" his dog said, miserably, and wandered off in a sulk.

"Are you coming out to play, Dermot?" asked Timmy, from next door.

"Sorry, I can't," said Dermot. "In case I get dirty."

Timmy went off to find someone else to play with.

Then his *mum* came outside.

"Can *you* empty the dustbin for me?" she asked. This was normally Dermot's favourite job.

"Sorry, I can't," he told her. "In case I get dirty."

Dermot's *mum* sighed. She hated emptying the smelly dustbin herself.

Next, Dermot's dad came out to do some gardening. He had to spread compost on his prize rhubarb. What a smell!

"Can you give me a hand?" he asked Dermot. "You love doing this sort of thing."

"Sorry, I can't," Dermot replied. "In case I get dirty."

His dad scowled, and put off the job until later.

Dermot was getting the fidgets. He'd been sitting still for far too long. He was hot and bothered and his shirt collar was too tight.

Aunt Clara sat down next to him.

"Now, isn't this nice?" she said.

Dermot didn't answer. He was watching his dad mow the lawn. There were grass clippings everywhere.

Suddenly, Aunt Clara gave a shriek.

"Look," she cried. "Ants! They're everywhere!"

She started slapping her legs and jumping up and down.

Then Dermot had an idea.

"I know how to get rid of ants," he told her. "Quick! Roll in those grass cuttings."

Aunt Clara did as she was told.

"Now, cover yourself in compost," said Dermot. "Ants hate compost."

Aunt Clara covered herself in compost and tried to shake off all the ants.

Dermot's dad stopped mowing. His mum came outside to see what all the fuss was about. They couldn't believe their eyes.

Aunt Clara looked a terrible sight. Her best dress was filthy. She was dirty and muddy, and covered in compost from head to toe. Her hair looked as if a bird had been nesting in it.

But at least she'd got rid of all the ants!

Everybody laughed. Except Aunt Clara. She made an excuse and hurried off home.

Dermot emptied the dustbin for his mum. He played ball with Timmy and his dog. Then he helped his dad with the compost.

"I never knew that rolling in grass cuttings and covering yourself in compost could get rid of ants," said Dermot's dad.

"Neither did I," chuckled Dermot. "Especially not very large aunts called Clara!"

also available...

Rude Roger   Dirty Dermot   Pickin' Peter   Space Alien Spike   Silly Sydney   Nude Nigel
Shy Sophie   Cute Candy   Royal Rebecca   Grown-up Gabby   Terrible Twins   Show-off Sharon